OAKIE DOKE
and the
Lonely Mouse

BBC CHILDREN'S BOOKS

Early one morning in Oakie Hollows, Oakie Doke's doorbell rang very loudly. Oakie Doke got out of bed and opened the door of his tree-house, yawning widely.

"Wh–what's happening?" he mumbled. "Who's there?"

He stepped sleepily on to his helter-skelter and slid down to see who wanted to talk to him so early in the morning.

"Whoo! Whee!" cried Oakie. He shot down the slide, going faster and faster. The wind whistled past his ears and by the time he reached the bottom, he felt wide awake.

"Hello, Rain Squirrel," said Oakie. "Was it you ringing my doorbell?"

"Yes," replied Rain. "I'm sorry to bother you so early in the morning, but I've got a bit of a problem."

"A problem?" said Oakie. "Well, you've come to the right place."

Oakie smiled. "What is your problem, Rain?"

"Well, it's not so much *my* problem as . . .
oh, dear," said Rain. "How can I explain? I think
you'd better come with me."

And Rain took him to her home in Oakie Haven.

Rain started to explain the problem when they reached Oakie Haven.

"Rufus and I were up early this morning," she began. "We wanted to show little Hazelnut the sunrise, you see."

"Did he enjoy it?" asked Oakie.

"It's hard to say, really," said Rufus. "He slept right through it!"

Oakie laughed.

Just then, the door of the Squirrels' house opened and a very shy mouse came out.

"Who's this?" asked Oakie in surprise.

"That's what I've been trying to tell you," said Rain. "This is Hickory. We found him early this morning."

"Hello, Hickory," said Oakie. "Well, you're a fine-looking young shrew!"

"I'm not a shrew," said Hickory. "I'm a mouse!"

"But you haven't got a tail," said Oakie. "You can't be a mouse."

"I *am* a mouse!" Hickory insisted tearfully. "I just haven't got a tail."

Oakie Doke nodded wisely.

"I understand," he said. "You're a very special mouse. After all, it's not every day that you meet a mouse without a tail."

"Where do you live?" asked Oakie.
"Nowhere," sniffed Hickory.
"I haven't got a home."
Oakie was shocked. "But what about your mum and dad?"
A big tear rolled down Hickory's face.

10

"No mum and dad either?" said Oakie, gently.
"Well, well, well. In that case, we'll just have to find
you a home, won't we!"

Hickory smiled hopefully, and Oakie took him
to Oakie Roots where Rose Corncracker and her
family lived.

Rose Corncracker was hanging out her washing when Oakie arrived.

"Hello, Oakie!" she called.

"Hello, Rose, hello, Albert," said Oakie. "This is Hickory."

Just then, Root and Snoot Corncracker came running up. They were playing tag.

"Tag!" shouted Root, tagging Hickory. "You're on!" Hickory laughed and chased after Root and Snoot. "Tag!" he cried, catching Snoot.

"Gosh," said Snoot, "you're a fast runner." She wasn't very happy about being caught.

"Still, I can see why," she said.

"Why?" asked Hickory.

"Because you've got no tail. You look more like a shrew than a mouse!" she said, rudely.

Hickory was very upset indeed. He turned round and started to walk away.

Snoot ran up to him and tagged him. "Tag!"

But Hickory didn't feel like playing any more, and he carried on walking sadly away.

"Spoil-sport!" shouted Snoot, and ran off.

The grown-ups soon noticed that Hickory was missing.

"Where has he gone?" asked Oakie.

"I don't know," said Root. "He ran away when Snoot said he looked just like a shrew."

"Snoot Corncracker," said Rose, sternly. "Were you making fun of him?"

"Only a bit," said Snoot.

"Dear me," said Oakie. "He's a little bit sensitive, you know."

"I'm sorry," said Snoot.

"Never mind," said Oakie. "We'll just have to find him."

Oakie Doke set off to look for the little mouse. "Hickory!" he called. "Hickory!"

"You'd better start looking for Hickory too, Snoot," said Rose. "And when you find him, you'd better say you're sorry!"

"I will," promised Snoot.

She set off to find Hickory. "Hickory! I didn't mean it!" she called. "Hickory!"

Snoot felt ashamed that she'd upset Hickory, and she hunted everywhere for him.

"Hickory!" she called. "I'm sorry! I didn't mean to be horrid!"

But suddenly, Snoot cried out in pain.

"Ouch! My tail's stuck!"

Snoot tried and tried to pull her tail free, but it was stuck fast.

"My tail! Oh, it hurts!" she said, and started to cry. "Help! Help! My tail's stuck! Someone, please help!"

Meanwhile, Hickory was walking along on his own, feeling very sad and lonely.

"It's not *my* fault I haven't got a tail," he said to himself.

Just then, he heard someone crying.

"It sounds like someone's hurt!" he said, and he ran off to see if he could help.

21

Hickory ran as fast as he could towards the cries.

"It's you!" he said in surprise, when he saw Snoot. "What's the matter?"

"I'm so pleased to see you, Hickory," said Snoot. "My tail's stuck and it hurts!"

"At least that's something *I* wouldn't have to worry about," said Hickory.

"Hickory, I'm so sorry about what I said. Really!" sobbed Snoot.

"That's all right," said Hickory, and he smiled at Snoot. "Now, let's see if I can get your tail free."

Hickory bent down and pulled at the tree root, trying very hard to be gentle.

"Ow!" cried Snoot in pain, as Hickory gave her tail a sharp tug.

But the very next moment, Snoot's tail was free.
"Oh, Hickory, you are clever! Thank you very, very much!" cried Snoot, giving Hickory a big hug.

Suddenly, the two mice heard a huge booming
noise.

"HICKOREE!"

It was so loud that they had to cover up their ears.

"Wow!" said Snoot. "That's Oakie Doke's voice. But
it's gone very loud!"

Sure enough, Oakie Doke appeared carrying an oak-leaf megaphone. His ears were stuffed with cotton-wool. "Very loud megaphone!" he shouted as he took the cotton-wool out of his ears.

"Still," he continued, "now that you've found Hickory, I won't need it any more."

"I didn't find him, Oakie," said Snoot. "He found *me*! I got my tail trapped and Hickory rescued me!"

"Well, I never!" said Oakie.

Back at Oakie Roots, Snoot told everyone how Hickory had rescued her.

"It seems we owe you some thanks for helping Snoot, young Hickory," said Rose. "Is there anything we can do to help *you*?"

"As a matter of fact, I think there is," said Oakie.

"You see, Hickory hasn't got a family," explained Oakie.

"Then he'd better come and live with us," said Rose. "We've got plenty of room, and Root has always wanted a brother."

"Oh, *yes!*" said Root.

29

"Please stay, Hickory!" cried Snoot.

"Yes, please do," begged Root. "Please!"

"What, even though I haven't got a tail?" said Hickory.

"Silly!" said Rose, as Root and Snoot joined hands with their new brother.

"Hooray!" said Oakie. "It's like I always say:
        A cat's not a dog
        And a sprat's not a whale,
        And you can't tell a mouse
        By a glance at his tail!"

Also published by BBC Children's Books:

Oakie Doke and the Nut Mystery

Published by BBC Children's Books
a division of BBC Worldwide Limited
Woodlands, 80 Wood Lane, London W12 0TT

First published 1995

Stills photography by Joe Dembinski

ISBN 0 563 40407 8

Based on the Television series produced by Cosgrove Hall Films Limited

Typeset by BBC Children's Books
Colour separations by Dot Gradations, Chelmsford
Printed and bound in Great Britain by Cambus Litho, East Kilbride

Frogs and Toads

Christine Butterworth and Donna Bailey

MACMILLAN

Have you ever heard frogs or toads
croaking in the night?
You might hear some bullfrogs or some
male toads croaking to call the females.

Frogs have a pouch of skin
under their chins.
They fill this pouch with air
to make their croak sound louder.

The male bullfrog croaks to warn
other males to keep away from
his patch of ground.
He will fight another bullfrog who
comes onto his patch.

This Australian water-holding frog
lives in the desert.
It stores water inside its body.
The Aborigine people squeeze the frog
to get water to drink.

This is a poison arrow frog.
South American Indians use these frogs
to poison their arrows.
The bright colours on its skin
warn birds that the frog
is not good to eat.

Tree frogs are small and thin.
They have sticky pads on their long toes
to help them cling to the trees.

Tree frogs can change the colour of
their skins to hide from their enemies.
A tree frog has a green skin when
it sits on a leaf.
The skin changes to brown when
it sits on the bark of a tree.

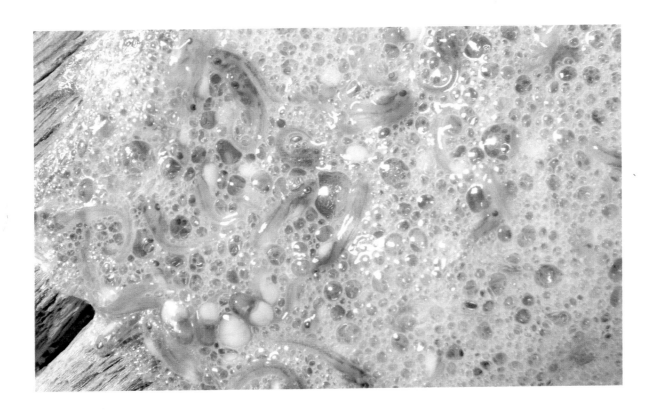

The female tree frog makes a frothy nest
for her eggs.
She beats the jelly around the eggs
into a froth.
The tadpoles grow in the middle
of the froth.

The male Darwin frog swallows
the eggs which the female lays.
The tadpoles grow inside his body.
After two months he opens his mouth and
out hop the little black baby frogs!

Toads look like frogs but
they are often fatter.
Toads have short back legs so they walk.
They do not jump like frogs.

A toad's skin is rough and dry and
has bumps all over it.
Toads spend most of their time on land.
They eat insects, slugs and snails.

Toads live in holes in the ground.

They stay there to keep cool during the day.

At night they come out to catch their food.

This spadefoot toad lives in a hole
in the hot desert.
It digs the hole with its back foot.
This foot has a hard edge of skin like
a spade for digging.

14

The spadefoot toad stays underground
out of the sun until the rains come.
It can stay in the earth without food
for more than a year!

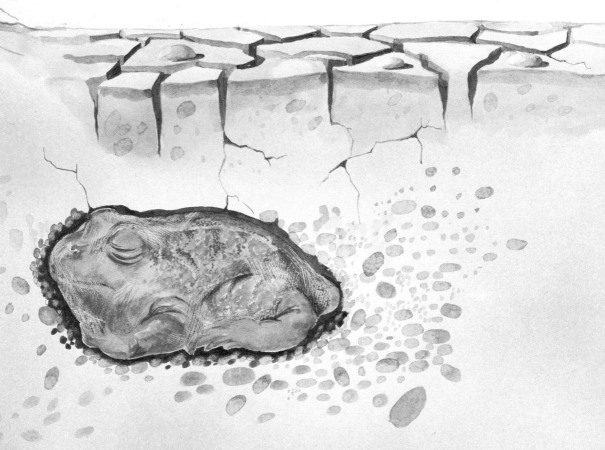

Index